Mary Dow Brine

Grandma's Attic Treasures

A story of old-time memoires

Mary Dow Brine

Grandma's Attic Treasures
A story of old-time memoires

ISBN/EAN: 9783337218379

Printed in Europe, USA, Canada, Australia, Japan

Cover: Foto ©Andreas Hilbeck / pixelio.de

More available books at **www.hansebooks.com**

GRANDMA'S

ATTIC TREASURES

A STORY OF OLD-TIME MEMORIES

By MARY D. BRINE

ILLUSTRATED

NEW YORK

E. P. DUTTON AND COMPANY

31 WEST 23D STREET

1886

ILLUSTRATIONS

Designed by

MISS C. A. NORTHAM,

J. FRANCIS MURPHY,

W. P. SNYDER.

EDMUND H. GARRETT,

W. A. ROGERS,

W. F. HALSALL

The book is prepared and the illustrations engraved

BY GEORGE T. ANDREW.

List of Illustrations.

GRANDMA'S ATTIC TREASURES.

————◆————

THERE, give me my knittin', dearie,
    It's somethin' I can't abide,
To set with my old hands idle,
    Like driftin' along on the tide.
I ain't so young as I once was,
    But there's one thing sartain sure
To rust out of life, as some folks do,
    Is a habit I can't endure.

Wal, yes, it is strange how time does fly;
    'Most takes one's breath away:
A creetur is hardly born, it seems,
    Afore she turns old and gray.
But I don't complain; for, if I 've seen
    A sight of worry and care,
There 's been a plenty of sunshine,
    And I s'pose I 've had my share.

Did I use to have beaux? Yes, plenty,
    And likely young fellows, too:
But I was full of my fun then, —
    As much of a witch as you
Are now, with your face so pretty,
    And your ways so dainty and fine;
But the beaux you girls have now-days
    Never were found in mine.

But I was a bit particular;

   So I and my heart were free

As ever the wind and summer air

   Till — Asa came courtin' me.

And, oh! I remember jest as plain

   How his blue eyes danced and shone

The day I promised him truly

   I'd be *his* sweetheart alone.

Of all the days that were glad and bright
I think the gladdest were then,
When Asa and I were lovers, dear,
And over and over agen
Kept makin' our plans for the future.
Come foul or sunshiny weather,
We used to say we did n't care which,
So that we shared it together.

But what did I promise to tell you
When you put me down in this cheer?
Oh yes, I remember now, dearie,
I know you wanted to hear
About the time of my sellin'
The things that folks call *antik*.
Wal, then, the mem'ry of that are time
E'enamost makes me sick.

Oh dear! shall I ever forget that day?
  The old man, Asa, had gone
Down to the fields for a load of hay,
  And I felt somehow forlorn
And kinder lonesome, and could n't tell why,
  As I stood there a-washin' dishes,
And lettin' my old, onruly heart
  Get full of onreasonable wishes.

You see I'd been wantin' a bunnit
   For nigh onto three good years;
And for shame of my shawl so faded
   I'd actually once shed tears;
And Asa *he* wanted a cow-critter
   Old Deacon Jones had to sell,
And — law! the half that we wanted
   I ain't got the patience to tell.

So I was a-wipin' my dishes,
   And now and then wipin' my eyes,
And grievin' over the shadows and clouds
   Which come to every one's skies,
Forgettin' the bright and sunny part,
   Which my eyes warn't willin' to see,
Because I thought at that minit
   They warn't shinin' bright for *me*, —

When all on a sudden there came a knock
  Right smart on the old front door;
(I did n't know when I had heard a sound
  Agen *that* door before).
So I tidied my hair at the kitchen glass,
  And smoothed my apern, and then
I nearly jumped out of my senses
  When the knock came soundin' agen.

But I went and opened it keerful,
  And I was amazed to see
Two stylish-lookin' gentlemen,
  And they bowed perlite to me.
There, now, if I'd been Victory,
  Those fellows could n't a been
A·bit perliter salutin' to me,
  Jest like if I'd been the Queen.

So I bowed back agen, of course,

My very best curtsy; for I

Was allers taught to be civil,

In the civil old days gone by.

And I said, says I, " Oh, how *do* you do?

Won't you kindly step in?"

(For I never *had* shet my door on folks,

And I wasn't a-goin' to begin.)

Wal, so they set down in the settin'-room,

And then they waited a bit;

For I was so flustered I scarcely knew

    What on airth to make of it.

But finally one of 'em said to me, —

    "Now, madam," says he, "I hear

That *you* have some antique furniture."

    Thinks I, "Law sakes! how queer!

"What on airth *does* he mean, I wonder!"

    But I said: "Oh, deary me!

I hain't no *antik* furniture,

    If it's that you're a-wantin' to see.

But what I've got is *powerful old*,

    And I'm sure it's cur'ous enough

Why anybody should want to see

    Sech a heap of worn-out stuff."

I noticed the men, they laughed at me,

 But there! I did n't keer;

Thinks I, " There 's allers been lots of fools,

 And a couple of 'em are here."

For cur'ouser folks I never see,

 A peekin' and pryin' about

As if there was n't an *airthly* thing

 They did n't want to find out.

Wal, arter a spell, when they 'd got through

 A-meddlin' with my affairs,

And I was a-tryin' to get 'em down

 A-past the garret stairs,

One of 'em spoke, and said, " Hold on,

 There 's one more place to go;

You 'll let us visit your garret, ma'am,

 Only a minit, you know."

Wal, there! I *was* 'most beat, my dear;
   But at once to myself says I,
" It 's plainer still that the day for fools
   Ain't anywhere nigh gone by!"
I could n't help but laugh, you know,
   For I never heard tell afore
Of two sech pecul'ar strangers.
   Says I, " There ain't no more

" That 's wuth your lookin' at, Mister,
   A heap of rubbidge and sich,
Old beds and cheers and tables,
   You can't tell t' other from which.
And I do feel mighty ashamed to show
   Such homely old trash, you see,
And they ain't no airthly use to a soul,
   So you better leave 'em be!"

But, dearie, would you believe it?

    What did they up and say,

But that they 'd ruther have *old* things

    Than new ones, any day !

So, — wal, I let 'em look at the duds —

    But what they wanted to do

Was somethin' I could n't onderstand,

    No more, I reckon, could you.

But by and by, when we got down stairs,

    The men they whispered a bit,

And then they said, " Now, madam, look here,

    If you 're willin' to part with it,

We 'll buy your furniture, such as we like,

    And give you a good, fair price."

I looked at them two poor lunatics,

    And my laugh riz up in a trice.

But I kinder smothered it down, for there,

  Thinks I, " I 've hearn of folks

Who hain't much else to do on airth

  But jest to be playin' jokes ! "

So I asked 'em kindly, " What did you say ?

  You 're willin' to buy of me

A part of my cheers and tables,

  And t' other old truck you see ? "

They bowed perlite, and answered,

  " Yes, certainly, ma'am," said they.

Said I, " Wal, I don't hardly know

  What Asa, my man, would say.

But s'posin', you call agen," says I,

  " And I 'll think of the matter some ;

You see I dunno jest what to say

  When father is n't to home."

With that, they went away at once,

   And I could n't but laugh to think

I 'd only to say the word, you know,

   And jest as quick as a wink

I could have my bran new bunnit,

   My new green shawl and all,

And Asa could have that cow-critter

   Along in the airly fall.

Wal, pretty soon Asa came along,

   All tired and tuckered out

With turnin' the hay in the medder,

   And drivin' the oxen about.

And down he set in the old arm-cheer,

   A-leanin' his gray old head

Agen the back. And he drew a breath,—

   " It is *good to rest !* " he said.

" Ay, Hannah, wife, it is good to rest,

   And it's better still to see

Your dear old face a-smilin' so sweet,

   And waitin' to welcome me.

I 'm gettin' along, old woman, you know

   And easily tired, my dear,

And arter all, there's nothin' like home

   And a comf'table easy cheer!"

Now, would you believe it, those men had chose
  That partickler cheer, and I
Was puzzled to death, when I looked at it,
  To know the reason why.
For a homelier thing I never did see,
  As plain as a pipe-stem, too;
I was so beat when they p'inted it out,
  I did n't know what to do.

Howsomever, I thought I would let it go,
  For I had n't s'posed Asa 'd keer;
Knowin' how many old things we had,
  I did n't have thought nor fear   ·
That he 'd say a word; but hearin' him speak
  In *that* way, it made me sad;
For, thinks I, " If he knows I 'm willin' to sell,
  It 'll make him sorter feel bad."

But I had to tell; and so I laid
My hand on his dear old head,
And kind of coaxin' like, said I,
" Asa, my dear," I said,

" The garret is full of old truck, you know,
Old truck that we never use,
And I'm thinkin' I'd like to sell 'em off,
And I s'pose *you* won't refuse?"

Dear! how he laughed! "Why, Hannah, wife,
  Who'll buy it, do you s'pose?
The like of our worn-out furniture
  Every soul in the village knows.
No, no, my woman, there's no one here
  You can cheat into thinkin' it's new;
It ain't so harnsome as once it was,
  But we'll have to make it do."

Then I up and told him the story,
  And told him about the men.
And how I had said I'd think it o'er,
  And they were a-comin' agen.
And I said, to him, "Now, father, dear,
  There's Deacon Jones' critter, you see,
You've wanted to buy her so long, my dear,
  Now here's your chance; and for *me*,

" I can have that bunnit I 'm wantin'.

   And won't be ashamed, you know,

To hold up my head among folks,

   When next Sabbath to meetin' we go!"

And I smoothed his forehead a little,

   And coaxed till my dear old man

Jest give me a kiss, and said, " Wal, dear,

   I 'm willin' to sell, if you can."

Wal, next day. bright and airly,

   When husband was goin' away,

He stopped to the barn-yard fence
  A minit or so, jest to say,—
"You 're *sure* you 're wantin' to sell the things?
  Don't go and be hasty, wife!"
And then he came back and kissed me.
  Wal, dearie, to save my life

I could n't see thro' my glasses
  For the tears that were dimmin' 'em so,
As I stood in the kitchen doorway
  A-watchin' the old man go

But 't warn't very long afore some one came,

Knockin' agen at the door,

And them two men stood there a-bowin',

Jest as on the day before.

The fust thing they asked me to sell 'em

Was Asa's old favorite cheer;

But you 'll laugh when I tell you I saw him

A-settin' into it, my dear,

As plain as if really he 'd been there,

And, law sakes! I 'll honestly say

It seemed as tho' if they 'd took the chair,

They 'd a-taken my man away.

For a picter came quickly afore me

Of how he did like to rest

(And finally get to snorin'

With his chin down low on his breast)

In that homely old cheer they wanted;
    And I got to thinkin', you know,
Of how that cheer was a part of ourselves
    In the days of the long ago.

For I could n't forget the time, ah, no,
    To go further back a good bit
(Altho' you saucy young witch
    May set there a-laughin' at it),
When all alone in our own snug home,
    My husband with me on his knee
Would sit with our arms 'round each other,
    Happy as we could be.

And the time that followed, you know, dear,
    When merry as bees in clover
Our little ones, restless and sturdy,
    Had clambered the old thing over;

And father, he 'd set there a-laughin' —
    Ah me! the picter was plain,
With the babies a-settin' upon his knee,
    Over and over agen.

So I said to the men, "Not that, sir,
    For I can't let it go!"
With that they looked at me quite surprised;

But I up and told 'em, you know,

How Asa had allers loved that cheer,

And thinkin' the matter o'er,

I guessed we 'd keep it till he had gone

Where cheers warn't needed no more.

Wal, when we came to the garret

They found a bedstead. (You see,

I 'd long ago tucked it away up there,

For it warn't any use to me.)

As plain and old and ugly a thing

As ever was made. But there!

As soon as *they* wanted to take it,

'T was somethin' I could n't spare.

For the tears that were dimmin' my spectacles

Could n't shet out the sight

Of the dear little heads that had lain there

For many and many a night,

So warm and snug on the pillow

In that very same little bed,

After each darlin' had lisped a prayer,

And the last good-night was said.

I polished my specs a little,

And then I says to the men,

" I reckon we won't decide 'bout that

Until I see you agen.

For there's many a thing comes afore me
  To hinder its goin' away;
And so long as there ain't no hurry,
  I'll think on 't another day."

Wal, they went on with their lookin'
  From one thing to another,
Pokin' and rummagin' all around,
  And forever a-nudgin' each other,
Till at last they spied in a corner
  A spinnin'-wheel. "*Massay!*" I said,
" If you 're thinkin' of buyin' *that* ere thing,
  You *must* be out of your head!"

Says one of 'em, "Madam, that's somethin'
  We very much want, and make bold
To ask you to sell it." "Oh, lawful sakes!"
  Said I, "now ain't it *tew* old?"
They shrugged their shoulders a mite, and then
  They laughed a minit or two,
And one of 'em said, "We'll buy it, ma'am,
  If it's all the same to you."

Says I, "Young man, be you married?
  Does your wife know how to spin?"
"Married!" laughed he, "now that's a scrape
  I haven't yet got in!"
I didn't exactly know what he meant,
  But I thought I'd let him know
That *spinnin'* had gone out of fashion
  Ever so long ago.

"I'm willin' to sell it, Mister,
　　But I feel it a dooty to say
That this 'ere spinnin'-wheel ain't no use,
　　And will only be in your way.
But law, if you really want it,
　　If you're set on havin' the thing,
I dunno but you're welcome,
　　For the sake of the price it'll bring."

So they marked it down in their book,
　　And, lookin' round a little more,
They diskivered a queer old table
　　A-standin' behind the door.
The oddest-lookin' table
　　That ever was seen, I declare,
And there did n't seem no reason
　　Why *that* thing I could n't spare.

It was sort of convenient in one way,
  It pulled out as fur as you chose,
And shet agen as small and snug
  As you please. Why, ev'ry one knows
Them tables went out of fashion
  Longer ago, I reckon, dear,
Than most folks now can remember, —
  'T was nigh onto eighty year,

Yes, nigh onto eighty year, I 'm sure,
  If it was a single day,
When those pryin' creeturs diskivered it,
  And wanted to take it away.
For Asa's folks had owned it
  Afore I married their son;
And among the presents they give us,
  That 'ere table was one.

Thinks I, " They may as well have it,"

  So they writ it down in their book.

And — wal, I hain't time to tell ye

  Of all those men *would* 'a' took

If I 'd only give 'em the chance.

  But I got so clean tuckered out,

That I hardly knew for sartain

  What on airth I *was* about.

So at last they whispered together,

  And one of 'em says, says he,

" Will fifty dollars pay you

  For the things we 've chosen ? "   Law me !

I could n't believe my senses ;

  But I felt in a sorter flurry,

And I told 'em yes, and then, my dear,

  They went away in a hurry,

And left me a-standin' and lookin'

At a big bill there in my hand;

And I tell you, child, it did look good,

And I felt consid'rable grand.

All *that* for a lot of rubbidge?

Ah, deary me! I *never*!

And I could 'a' kept on lookin'

And wonderin' on it forever!

Wal, the money I put in the stockin'

Atop of the kitchen shelf,

And the very fust chance I had to think
  A minit all to myself,
Says I, " I 'll jest step to the garret
  And dust off them things a bit."
Oh my! how flustered and queer I felt
  The minit I thought of it!

So, arter I 'd gone to the garret,
  And began a-dustin', wal, there!
I had the pecul'arest feelin's
  Take holt of me, I declare!
I looked at the spinnin'-wheel, dearie,
  And somehow, I could n't tell why,
Before I hardly could help it
  I was e'enamost ready to cry.

There warn't nobody to see me,
  And I felt mighty glad,

For ev'rything seemed possest to
  make
My old heart troubled and sad.

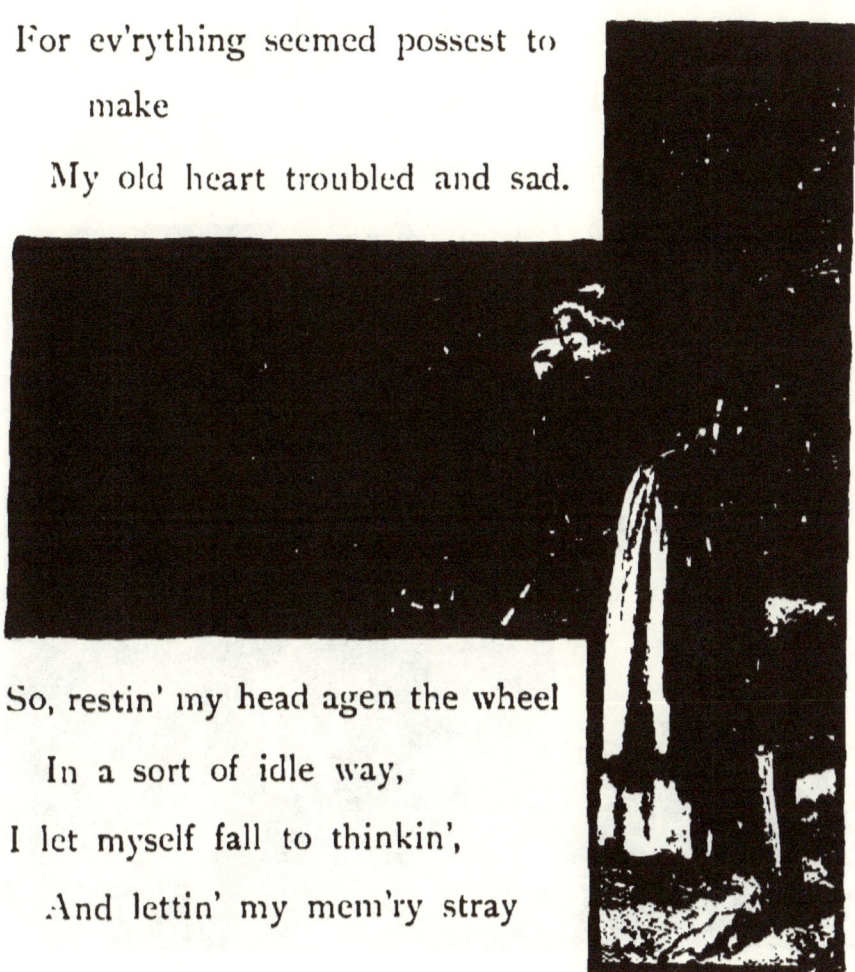

So, restin' my head agen the wheel
  In a sort of idle way,
I let myself fall to thinkin',
  And lettin' my mem'ry stray

To the time when I was a slip of a gal
  A-wearin' Asa's ring,
Too happy to do a thing all day
  But laugh and chatter and sing.

And I minded the times the wheel went round
  To the merry tunes I sung,
In the days when skies were *allers blue*,
  'Cause Asa and I were young.

There was many a lovin' secret
  That I told to my wheel, my dear,
With the blushes a-burnin' on my cheek,
  Tho' nobody else was near,

    As out on the farm-house porch I spun
      In the pleasant summer weather,
    Weavin' many a hank of thread
      And gay romance together.

But there came a lover's quarrel, child,

   A quarrel 'twixt Asa and me,

And oh! the days, the mis'rable days,

   When his face I did n't see!

How did it happen? Wal, I forget,

   It was all so long ago;

But there! young tongues are hasty of speech,

   And so were ours, I know.

How long did it last? Oh, wal, my child,

   It really appeared to me

That minits were fairly hours,

   And the days seemed *weeks* to be!

I turned my wheel with a laggard foot,

   And I had no heart for song;

And try as I might, it seemed as tho'

   My work was bound to go wrong.

But one bright day, I remember,

    When ev'rythin' seemed so glad

That it looked as if I was the only one

    Of God's creeturs who was sad,

I was settin' afore my spinnin'-wheel,

    But the wheel was movin' so slow

That it did n't amount to nothin',

    And finally ceased to go;

For I dropped my hands in my lap,

    And I let my foot from the treadle fall,

And I set jest idly thinkin',

    And seein' nothin' at all,

Except the face I was carryin'

    In my heart from mornin' till night,

And holdin' fast in my dreams

    Till once again it was light.

Wal, as I was settin' there lonely like,

With many a tear on my cheek,

Somebody's hands went over my eyes, —

Ah! not a word did he speak.

But I *knew* it was no one but Asa,

And my heart got a-beatin' so fast

I could n't move or say nothin'

Till arter a spell was past;

But I lifted my hands from my lap,

    And I clasped 'em over his own,

And the tears they came like raindrops;

    And not only *my* tears alone.

For I felt the tears from my lover's eyes

    A-splashin' agen and agen

On the back of my hand, as he bowed his head,

    And kissed my forehead; and then —

Ah, wal, no matter what followed;

    But till the sun was low in the west

We sang together, my heart and I,

    And — law! you can guess the rest.

For Asa called round in the evenin',

    And we talked our trouble away,

And there hain't been another quarrel

    'Twixt us since that glad day.

Wal, you see I was thinkin' of all those things
  That day in the garret, and so
I kinder hated the promise I'd give
  To let the old wheel go.
But I dusted it off and fixed it up,
  For says I to myself, "I'm sure,
To break a promise once made 's a thing
  Hannah Spriggins can never endure!"

Then I went to the table to dust it off,
  And tidy *that* up for the men,
Till those same cur'us feelin's possest me,
  And dimmed my glasses agen.
That table! I minded when my old man
  Sot to it alone with me
(When he warn't *old* by a sight of years)
  A-drinkin' his cup of tea.

There was only *two* of us then, you know,
    For I was a bit of a wife,
And never a thought of trouble or care
    Could hurt my giddy young life.
I allers did my own cookin',
    And husband, he praised me well,
And I was proud of our little home,
    Prouder than words could tell.

Then by and by, when the babies came
    To open our hearts yet more,

We made the table larger a bit, —
  Large enough to hold *four*.
For the little fellers they grew so fast,
  The two little dimpled dears,
That it warn't *no* time afore they set
  To the table in little high cheers.

Yes, they were twins, them fust that came,
  And nobody ever see
Sturdier, smarter babies than them
  That belonged to father and me.

But sorrow came, and — wal, we made
    That table small as before,
And it almost broke our hearts to know
    We were *only two* once more.

Wal, time went on, and 't was quite a spell
    'Fore we lengthened it out again.
But there came at last to the lonely house —
    To lift its burden of pain —
The blessed sound of sweet voices,
    So dear to a mother's ear,
And the laugh of my growin' children
    Was glad and pleasant to hear.

And then my man and I we pulled
    That table to sech a size
As gladdened our hearts, you may be sure,
    And gladdened our lovin' eyes.

Law! sech a row of the little heads!
　Black and yaller and brown!
We used to think them babies of ours
　Were jest the nicest in town.

But have n't you noticed, dearie,
　Sometimes on a summer's day,
When there ain't a cloud to be seen in the sky,
　And as fur as you look away
Over the hills and medders
　The sunshine seems so bright,
It seems as tho' 't would be allers day,
　And there warn't sech a thing as *night?*

Wal, that is how it appeared to me,
And I never once dreamed of sorrow;
Bein' so pleased with the present day,
I could n't think of the morrow,
Nor give a thought to the sartain fact
That a *night must* lie between
Two days, you know, no matter if they
Are the brightest ever seen.

And so when the shadows gathered,
They caught me unprepared,
And of many homes by a fever robbed,
Our dear home was not spared.
And father and I awoke one day
From a long, unconscious rest,
To find our darlin's, our own dear birds,
Had flown from the old home nest.

And he and I were again alone,

    Just as we were afore,

Just as we 'd been, you see, dear,

    At the very fust start.   Once more

We pushed the table together,

    And at every meal we two

Felt so heart-sick and lonely

    We scarcely knew what to do.

And at last I could n't a-bear it,

    And I said to Asa one day,

" I wish," said I, " you 'd let me put

    This table out of the way;

And s'posin' you trade for another

    That ain't so lonely as this."

My man, he pondered a minit,

    Then came and give me a kiss.

"Ay, Hannah, you're missin' the babies!
　Wal, there *is* too much of space
In this old house, dear wife, I know,
　At best, it's a lonesome place!
But it's holdin' *you* yet, thank Heaven,
　And, please God, it'll hold you long,
And spare your man, my dearest,
　To work for you good and strong."

So 'twarn't long arter, it happened
　He traded a load of hay,
And brought me home from market-town
　A bran-new table one day.
And I put the old one clean out of sight,
　And forgot it arter a while,
'Specially when a *new* baby came,
　And we learned agen to smile.

And all the years it had stood there,

Gettin' so awful old, you see,

Our one little baby was growin'

A pretty young gal to be.

At fifteen she was a beauty,

At sixteen the village belle ;

And—my! the half of her lovers

I'm sure I never can tell.

Wal, a likely young feller came to us,

And courted her up and down,

And the end of it was she married him,

And went to live in his town.

And soon he took her to foreign parts,

And made her so grand and fine

You 'd scarcely believe she 'd ever been

A darter of Asa's and mine.

Oh, yes! she kept on livin' there

For many a month. And then

It happened one day when Asa had gone

Down to the fields with the men,

There came a letter for him and me,

And these are the words it said:

" A daughter was born last week to us,

To-day her *mother lies dead !* "

I did n't get no farther, child,
  For I fainted clean away,
And Asa was fetched from the medder,
  And for many a weary day
He nussed me keerfully, dearie,
  But oh! it was long afore
I could dry my eyes from their weepin'
  For the darter I 'd see no more.

They kept the baby in toreign parts
  Where its father's relations were,
And the child knew 'bout as little of *me*
  As I ever heard of *her*.
But I could n't help thinkin' all the same
  That things might come about
So that *somewhere* on the face of the airth
  I 'd find my grandchild out.

But I 'm wanderin' off my subject,
  Let 's see — wal, about the bed.
I went to that next to dust it,
  And, " I won't be foolish!" I said;
So I stood beside it detarmined
  To forget the past. But there!
There was no use fightin' agen it,
  For law! dear, I declare,

As I stood there lookin' down on it,
  For all the time passed away,
For all I had turned an old woman,
  Wrinkled, bony, and gray,
Yet still thro' the mist on my glasses,
  And thro' mist of the years long gone,
I could see my lost ones before me,
  As long ago, in the morn

Of my motherhood, gladsome and happy,
  When the twins — little Asa and Ben —
Had played from the dawnin' of daylight
  Till came the gloamin', and then

I would gather 'em close in my arms
  Till the droopin' of each golden head
Would make father remind me, " Come, mother,
  You 'd better jest snug 'em in bed."

Ah me! wal, you 've hearn how the Shepherd
   That loves little lambs, thought it best
To call *my* lambkins to heaven
   In his own lovin' arms to find rest.
So the bed, for a spell it lay empty,
   Till came Hiram and Eben, and soon
Two more little fellers a-claimin'
   A share in the lullaby tune.

Laws! how that bed kept a-stretchin'
   Like rubber to hold jest one more,
Until I went up ev'ry evenin'
   To kiss and say good-night to four
Little frolicksome, rosy-cheeked youngsters
   All liftin' their dear arms to me,
A-tryin' to hug and kiss mother
   Ahead of each other, you see.

Wal, how could I help it, now, dearie,

    If while I stood thinkin' that day

Of the forms and the sweet baby faces

    So long, oh, so long passed away,

These foolish old eyes of mine weakened,

    And at last I jest dropped my head,

And givin' a sob I could n't keep back,

    " Oh, babies! *my* babies!" I said,

"Only jest for one minit to see ye

    A-lyin' so merry and bright,

And waitin' for mammy to kiss ye,

    My darlin's, for sweet good-night!

Only jest for *one* hour of havin'

    Ye all to myself once more!

I 'd love ye, I 'd kiss ye, my babies,

    As never I kissed ye afore!

"Only jest to be able to kneel

With my cheek agen yours, my dears,

A-hearin' ye lispin' your prayers once more!

Ah me! I'm thinkin' my tears

Would all be a-turnin' to di'monds

With the smiles that would shine in my eyes,

Jest like as the dewdrops sparkle

In the sun of the mornin' skies."

Oh, wal, it warn't no use frettin',

  And I thought, arter all, 't would be best

To forget all about the old treasures

  And let the bed go with the rest.

So, arter I 'd left the garret

  I went to the settin'-room

And drew up the winder curtains

  To lighten the twilight's gloom.

And next day, bright and quite airly

  (I 'd almost hoped they 'd be late),

Two men came drivin' a waggin

  Close alongside of our gate.

(Father had gone an hour afore),

  Says I to the men, " I s'pose

You 're wantin' to cart the duds away.

  They ain't wuth much, land knows,

But I'm kinder sorry I sold 'em."

"Wal, ma'am," said the man to me,

"I reckon you'll have to let 'em go,

A bargain's a bargain," says he.

So they h'isted 'em into the waggin,

And land! they worked so fast

That afore I knew it they driv away,

And — my things were gone at last!

Wal, arter their dust had settled down,

And my kitchen chores were done,

I looked at the empty places

Silently, one by one.

I'm free to confess I polished my specs,

(You know I allers do

When I'm the least mite flustered, —

Some day, dear, so may *you*.)

But I tried to keep up my sperrits
  Till dinner-time came, and then
(When Asa came home) I clean give up,
  And bust into tears agen.
My good man did n't say nothin' at fust,
  But he drew his cheer by me,
And puttin' his arm about my waist,
  He pulled me down on his knee.

" Hannah, old woman," he says to me,
  A-passin' his dear old hand
Over my cheek so lovin' like,
  As tho' he could onderstand
Jest how my heart was a-throbbin',
  By old-time memories stirred,
And he had to do all the talkin',
  For I could n't speak a word.

" Hannah, old woman," he says to me,
  " Thro' clouds and sunny weather
You and I, my dear old wife,
  Have been growin' old together.
Growin' old *together*, dear heart,
  Ay, spared to comfort each other,
And tho' our children are all asleep,
  We still are father and mother

" To sons who never will break *our* hearts
  With goin' their wilful ways
(Like that there boy of the Deacon's
  And the son of the Widder Hays).
We 're nearin' the harbor, ain't we, wife?
  And the children will ferry us o'er
The dark, deep river that we must cross
  To get to the happy shore.

" 'T would be hard to bear now, would n't it, wife,
  If one of us had to live
Without the comfort and lovin' care
  The other is ready to give.
If one of us slept with the children, —
  Wal, there! the dear Lord knows
That it will come 'most too hard on one
  Arter the other goes!

"So he keeps us trudgin' together, dear,
　Along on the way, and I
Am nowise afeard he 'll forget us
　Till it comes *our* turn to die.
Don't grieve no more o'er the things you sold,
　We needed the cash, I know,
And I guess, old woman, that you were wise
　Decidin' to let 'em go."

"Oh husband!" I said, a-dryin' my tears,
　"I wish there had n't a mite
Of the dear old stuff gone outer the house.
　I 'd give a deal for a sight
Of that plain old table! oh my! I 'm sure
　I must have been nigh *possest*,
To have spared that table and that there bed!
　I 'm full of grief and onrest

" With hankerin' arter them all agen I
    The empty places, you see,
Are, oh! *so* empty, dear Asa,
    They look so lonely to me !
Wal, there 's the money a-lyin'
    Atop of the kitchen shelf ;
Do take it out of my sight, my dear,
    For I 'm e'enamost sick of myself ! "

So, arter that a week went by
    Quiet and peaceful, and we
Were gettin' used to the spaces
    Where the old truck used to be.
I had my Sunday bunnit,
    And a harnsome new green shawl,
And Asa had the promise
    Of the Deacon's cow in the fall.

And then one day the Deacon driv
   Along beside our gate,
And hollered, " Hannah Spriggins !
   Be ye there ? Wal, I can't wait,
So be spry, for here's a letter,
   And I reckon it comes from York;
I thought I'd bring it along this way,
   But I hain't no time to talk."

I finished my work in the kitchen,

    A-wonderin', as you may guess,

Whoever on airth could have writ to *me*,

    And there, I 'm free to confess

I felt that nervous and flustered

    That I got in a presperation,

And thought of a hundred worriments

    That had n't got no foundation.

But I could n't feel ready to open it,

    For somehow I did n't keer

To read the letter jest then, you see,

    When father was n't near.

So I finished a-rollin' my dough out,

    And settin' my bread to bake,

And I tried to forget the letter

    In a pie I had to make.

Wal, when we opened the letter,

   And read it keerful thro',

We both of us looked at each other, —

   I laughed, and Asa did, too.

Then right in the midst of our laughin'

   What did I do but cry?

While Asa, dear heart, I heard *him*

   A-heavin' a sort of sigh.

For what do you think! My grandchild

   Had come from foreign parts

With some of her fine relations,

   And the yearnin' prayer in the hearts

Of Asa and me, it seemed as tho'

   The Lord was willin' at last

To grant, and "grandma and grandpa's" love

   Was growin' sudden and fast.

The child expressed a desire to see
Her mother's early home. '
" Would grandma and grandpa," she wondered.
" Be willin' to let her come
To the dear old farm for two or three days
To get acquainted, before
Her uncle would have to take her back
To the distant English shore?"

Wal, when she came, law! dearie,

　　We could scarce believe our eyes!

It did n't seem as if Polly's child

　　Could have grown to sech a size!

A winsome lassie of sixteen year,

　　With her mother's bonny face,

And carryin', too, in all her ways,

　　Her mother's innocent grace.

I rubbed my specs till they shone so clear

　　I could n't make no mistake ;

Then I took her face between my hands,

　　And my heart was fit to break

With lookin' into the soft blue eyes

　　That were my dead Polly's own,

And hearin' my darter's voice agen

　　In my grandchild's merry tone.

And father, he kissed her agen and agen,

    Tho' he could n't find words to speak;

But he laid his wrinkled face, my dear,

    Agen her rosy young cheek.

"She's like her mother, dear wife," he said,

    "The child who played at our side

In the years agone, afore ever she dreamed

    Of bein' a rich man's bride."

How long did she stay?   Not long, oh no,
    For her folks they had to go
'Way back to their own fine home agen
    In foreign parts; and so
There came to the poor old farm at last
    A lonely, sorrowful day
When the child we loved gave her last sweet kiss,
    And turned from our home away.

And arter that a couple of years
    Went pleasant and peaceful by,
And Asa and me, we jogged along
    Under a shiny sky.
And there warn't no tribulations
    Nor trials, dearie, you see,
A-tarnin' up, as there had been once,
    A-botherin' Asa and me.

But durin' then my grandchild,

    She married a man; and then

She said good-by to English shores

    And came to York agen.

And, my! she lived so fash'nable,

    And grew so fine and grand,

I never could screw up courage —

    You 'll easily onderstand —

To go and stay to her house,

    As many a time she sent

An invite pressin' and hearty.

    But I 'd 'a' been glad to went

If I had n't 'a' had a feelin'

    That a plain old wrinkled creetur

With nothin' at all to brag on,

    Either in form or featur,

Would sorter be out of place

    Among things so harnsome and new.

And there was father, my poor old man!

    He 'd miss me sadly, I knew.

But then, I hankered to see her,

    My Polly's motherless darter;

And, wal, I finally said I 'd go,

    'Cause Asa, he said I oughter.

So I put my duds in the old hair trunk,

    And airly one pleasant day

Asa, he hitched up old Dobbin,

    And together we driv away

To the rail-keer station. Oh, massy sakes!

    How I did feel, my dear,

At partin' with Asa, for he and me 'd

    Kept close for nigh fifty year.

And now I was goin' to leave him!

    Wal, there, as I set at his side,

I'm free to confess, right straight in the road

    I presently up and cried.

But then old Miss Higgins had promised

    To look a bit arter my man,

And, "Asa, my dear," said I, "you know

    I'll come back as soon as I can!"

So at last I got into the steam-keer,

And Asa, he called to me:

"Good-by, old woman, take keer of yourself,

Hannah, dear heart!" called he.

And then there came a rushin' noise,

And my head felt dizzy and queer,

And thinks I to myself, "I'd give a sight

If I only *was n't here!*"

Wal, I got to my grandchild's house at last;

And, sakes! I was 'most beat

To see sech elegant carpits

Lyin' round under folks' feet!

And me a-walkin' onto 'em as if

They could n't be spiled, my dear,

And, law! if you'll believe me, child,

I did n't see *one cheer*

That I really darst to set down in

    For somehow it 'peared as tho'

They was powerful weak and brittle,

    Not a bit like *mine*, you know.

And there were a sight of figgers

    On marble stools and sich,

And a heap of confusin' gimcracks, —

    I did n't know which from which.

And the times I bumped my poor old head
  Agen a big lookin'-glass,
When I see a room where I wanted to go,
  A-tryin', you see, to pass
Right into it! for how could I tell
  'T was only a glass? and, law!
I never see sech deceivin' things
  In *my* born days afore!

But arter I 'd been a-visitin' there
  For nigh on a week, one day
I was kinder wanderin' round the house
  In a sort of homesick way,
When I see my darter in her boodoor,
  And she said to me, "Come in!"
So I went and set on the sofy.
  Wal, there! I can't begin

To tell the half of the furniture
   That was fillin' the place! Thinks I,
" It 's wuth a creetur's life to move,
   And I 'm sure I dassent try!"
So I went to knittin' on Asa's sock
   (It was in my pocket, you know;
I allers carry my knittin'-work
   Wherever I chance to go),

And Polly, she set a-readin',
   And we was as quiet as mice,
When all on a sudden I see a thing
   That riz me up in a trice.
It was only a little old table,
   All polished and shinin'; but law!
It looked amazin' like that I 'd sold
   To the men so long afore.

" Polly," says I, "ain't that there thing

A *little* bit out of place

In this here fine house of yours?" And then

She laughed right out in my face.

" That table, you mean? why, grandma,

That 's as old as the hills, you know!"

Says I, a-rubbin' my spectacles,

Says I, " Wal, yes, that 's so,

" For I had one amazin' like it,

And a lot more rubbidge, I sold

To a couple of crazy lunatics

Who wanted 'em 'cause they was old.

And you would n't believe two human souls

Would have actually paid me money

For cheers and tables and real old things ;

Now, Polly, was n't it funny !

" But they lugged 'em away, and it 'peared to me

   I missed 'em a sight. It 's queer

How that there table should make me think

   Of mine. But, Polly, my dear,

If I was *you*, when my fine friends call

   I 'd be 'shamed to have 'em see

A thing so out of fashion; it spiles

   Your room, it appears to me! "

With that I put my spectacles on

   To take a good look at the thing,

A-standin' right out conspicuous

　　With its drawers, and each brass ring

A-shinin' as bright as gold, my dear,

　　A-shinin' as bright as gold,

And lookin' as chipper and sassy

　　As tho' 'twarn't powerful *old.*

And there set Polly a-laughin';

　　But then, who keered, my dear?

Altho' she was thinkin' 'most likely

　　That grandmas was mighty queer.

For I suddenly did diskiver,

　　By a sartain familiar sign,

That that there table in Polly's room

　　Had long ago stood in mine.

It was jest my own dear table,

　　The one I had grieved for so long;

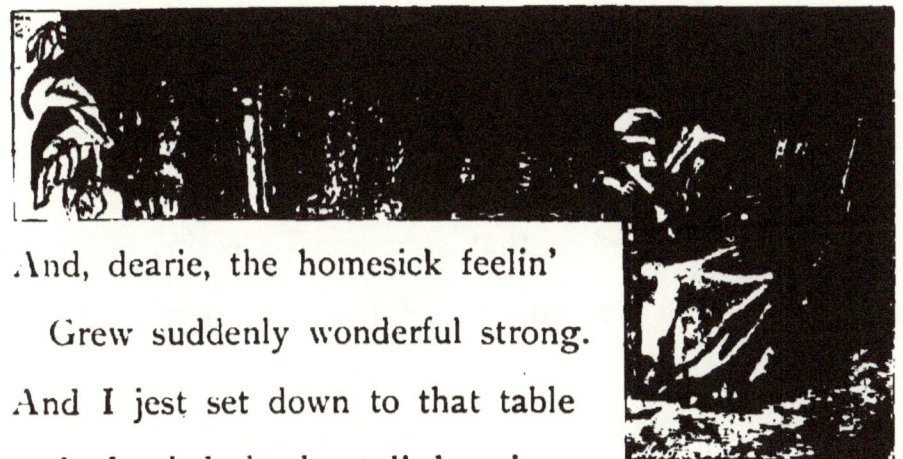

And, dearie, the homesick feelin'
  Grew suddenly wonderful strong.
And I jest set down to that table
  And cried the least little mite,
For them old brass rings that my babies had clutched
  Were good to my achin' sight.

Wal, arter Polly stopped laughin'
  She up and told me, dear,
Some funny things, I can tell you,
  I never expected to hear.
For she said there 'd been a powerful rage
  In New York town, you know,
For things folks called antik and sech,
  And "old as the hills," and so

The men who came pryin' to my house,
  A-meddlin' with things, were expectin'
To find big bargains to bring to York,
  For the store that sent 'em collectin'.
And I'm free to confess I was riled a mite
  To think they'd only paid *me*,
For all they had took, fifty dollars,
  And my grandchild had paid, you see,

For that there table alone, she said,
  Fifty dollars or more!
Wal, there! I was e'enamost beat, my dear,
  For in all my life afore
I had never heard tell of sech cheatin' men;
  My *Asa* warn't no sech kind!
And a cheatin', deceivin' creetur, child,
  Warn't never to *my* mind.

But the table, the dear old table!
   Oh, dearie, you surely know
How glad I was to get it again
   In my grandchild's house; and so
I writ to father that very night,
   And I told him, " Asa," says I,
" Our Polly, she says *new*-fashioned things
   Are all a-goin' by.

" *New*-fashioned times is behind the age,
   Old-fashioned things is new,
And things ain't new, or wuth a cent,
   Unless they 're *antik* too.
And the cur'ous part of it all, my man,
   Is a lesson I 'm larnin' well:
The duds stowed away these forty years
   Are too fash'nable to sell.

" But law! there's one thing puzzles me,
  And I'm wonderin', Asa dear,
If the world thinks any the more of *folks*
  Who are ruther antik and queer;
But there! I reckon that neither of us,
  My man, will ever be able
To prove *our* wuth compared with that
  Of a *valu'ble antik table.*"

But I didn't stay long at Polly's,
  For somehow I couldn't stay,
A-knowin' the old man missed me.
  So airly one pleasant day
My grandchild's husband took me
  To the keers, and we said good-by,
And I was so glad to be gettin' home,
  I was really afraid I should cry.

Wal, Asa was there at the station,

    A-waitin' and watchin' for me,

And as soon as the keers reached our village,

    His face was the fust thing I see.

So we rode in the waggin, side by side,

    Back over the road agen,

Till we neared the dear old home-

        stead

    Under the elms, and then

My man, he turned his face to me,

And the tears were in his eyes:

" Oh Hannah, wife, the sun has come

Straight back to the old home skies!

You 're welcome home, dear heart!" he said;

And he put a kiss on my cheek.

I kissed him back, but my heart was full,

And I did n't dare to speak.

Wal, we settled down agen at last

In the quiet old home together;

And whatever the gloom, whatever the shine

Of life, its wind and weather,

We shared alike, my man and me,

As, please God, to our old life's end

We may share together whatever of joy

Or grief he may choose to send.

There, now, you have heard my story,

   And Asa's stocking is done;

(Dear me! it is late — it's time he was back,

   And the medder is hot with the sun!)

Jest help me in on your arm, dear,

   And now, as you're goin' home,

I'll set to the winder awhile alone,

   And watch for Asa to come.

See! there he is by the pasture bars,
    A-wavin' his hand to me;
He *knows* I'm here by the winder
    A-watchin' for him, you see.
Wal, good-by, dearie; come often
    With your bright and bonny young face,
If you ain't afeard that amongst the *antik*
    Your style will be — out of place.